Goosebumps®

PRESENTS

Have you seen the new show on Fox Kids TV? It's creepy. It's spooky. It's funny. . . . It's GOOSEBUMPS!

Don't you love GOOSEBUMPS on TV? And if you do, then you'll love this book, *Night of the Living Dummy II*. It's exactly what you see on TV — complete with pages and pages of color photos right from the show! It's spook-tacular!

So check under your bed, pull your covers up tight, and start to read *Night of the Living Dummy II*. GOOSEBUMPS PRESENTS is so good . . . it's scary!

Look for more books
in the GOOSEBUMPS PRESENTS series:

Goosebumps®

PRESENTS

NIGHT OF THE LIVING DUMMY II

Adapted by Carol Ellis
From the teleplay by Rick Drew
Based on the novel by R.L. Stine

SCHOLASTIC INC.
New York Toronto London Auckland Sydney

A PARACHUTE PRESS BOOK

Adapted by Carol Ellis, from the teleplay by Rick Drew.
Based on the novel by R.L. Stine.

ISBN 0-590-74590-5

Photos courtesy of Protocol Entertainment © 1995
by Protocol Entertainment.
Text copyright © 1996 by Parachute Press, Inc.
All rights reserved. Published by Scholastic Inc.
GOOSEBUMPS is a registered trademark of Parachute Press, Inc.

12 11 10 9 8 7 6 5 4 3 2   6 7 8 9/9 0 1/0

Printed in the U.S.A.   40
First Scholastic printing, October 1996

"I call it 'Home Sweet Home,'" my older sister explained. She smiled and held up her painting. It looked like our house, a regular two-story house in the suburbs.

"Sara, that's just beautiful," Mom told her.

"It belongs in a museum," Dad added. "Nice work!"

It was Thursday night. Thursday night is always "Family Sharing Night" in the Kramer home. I'm not crazy about it, but Mom and Dad insist. They say it's a tradition we'll always remember.

This is the way it goes. We all get together in the living room. Then each member of the family has to present something to the rest of the family. It can be a story or a song or a joke or something we've made.

Sara almost always does a painting or a sketch. She's fourteen. She's a really good artist — and she knows it.

"I'm entering my painting in the city art show," she bragged, staring admiringly at her creation.

I rolled my eyes. "She showed us the exact same painting *last* Family Night," I muttered.

"Okay, who's next?" Dad asked. I started to get up out of my chair, but my brother, Jed, jumped up off the floor. "I'm next!" he shouted.

Jed's younger than I am. He's ten. He's a total goof. *And* a total pain.

"Amy, let Jed go," Dad said to me.

I flopped back down in my chair. I'm twelve. I'm the middle kid, and I hate it. Sara is smart and pretty and gets all the praise. Jed is cute and goofy and gets away with everything.

All I get to do is wait.

Jed grabbed the remote control and pointed it at the TV/VCR. "This week I'm going to show the video I made about us." He grinned and punched PLAY on the remote.

The TV screen lit up. Loud rock music blared from the speakers. Jed had even made a soundtrack.

We all stared at the television.

First we saw my mom, standing in front of the refrigerator. She glanced around, then stuck a huge spoonful of ice cream into her mouth.

"There's Mom," Jed narrated with a laugh. "Sticking to her diet again!"

Mom is always trying to lose weight. And Jed had caught her sneaking ice cream when she thought she was alone!

Mom blushed and gave Jed a little frown. She looked relieved when the scene changed.

Next the screen showed Dad sitting in the car. He was staring into the rearview mirror, playing with his hair.

Jed snickered. "And there's Dad, getting his hair just right!"

The thing is, Dad is almost bald. The "hair" he was fixing was really a toupee. He puts it on before he goes to work. Dad didn't know Jed was taping him while he did it that day.

Dad ran a hand over his shiny scalp. He blushed like Mom did.

The next part showed Sara. She didn't know Jed was taping her, either. She was posing in front of the bathroom mirror.

"Here's how come Sara hogs the bathroom so much!" Jed called out, laughing again.

I laughed, too. Sara had a ton of gooey makeup on her face. She kept turning her head and flipping her hair as if she were a fashion model.

"Jed, you're such a pain," Sara complained.

I kept laughing. But then the scene changed again. This time Jed had secretly been taping *me*!

"Guess whose new sweater Amy is trying on?" Jed asked.

There I was, sneaking into Sara's bedroom — trying on her new pale blue sweater.

"You little geek!" I screamed at Jed. I tried to wrestle the remote away from him.

"Amy, where's your sense of humor?" Dad asked.

"Yeah, Amy!" Jed cried. "I could send my tape to that TV show — *Fractured Family Videos* — and win a fortune!"

Sara glared at me. "How many times do I have to tell you not to try on my clothes?" she said. I couldn't really blame her for being angry.

Everybody was glad when the video ended. Mom frowned at Jed again. I could tell she was still embarrassed about being caught scarfing the ice cream. "That wasn't very nice, Jed. And you didn't ask permission to use the camera."

"Sorry," he murmured. Then he smirked at me and snuggled onto the couch with Mom and Dad. "Your turn, Amy."

It's about time, I thought. I sat down on the big padded footstool and reached for Dennis.

Dennis is a ventriloquist's dummy. A very

old dummy. The paint on his face is faded. He has shaggy brown hair, and his red turtleneck sweater is all worn out.

I have fun with Dennis. I'm not very good at talking without moving my lips. But I keep practicing.

I balanced him on my left knee and wrapped my fingers around the string in his back. The string makes his mouth move.

"So, Dennis, how was your family picnic?" I asked. Dennis and I always tell jokes. "Were you bothered by any ants?"

I pulled the string. "No — worse! We had termites!" Dennis answered in the high, shrill voice I use. "You've heard of the Terminator? Well, we had to call the Ex-terminator! Huh-huh-huh! Huh-huh-huh!"

I kept making laughing sounds and pulling on the string to make Dennis's mouth move. All of a sudden, Dennis's head fell off. It just slipped off his skinny shoulders. It hit the floor with a little thud and rolled to a stop.

Sara burst out laughing. So did Jed. "That was the best part!" he shouted.

"This is *so* embarrassing!" I cried to Dad. "You said I could get a new dummy!"

"So I did," Dad told me with a smile. "Why don't you look behind the couch?"

"Really? You really got me a new one?" I dropped Dennis the headless dummy and ran toward the couch.

"Well, almost new," Dad explained. "I was passing a second-hand store near my office. There he was. Just sitting in the window."

Behind the couch sat a small, beat-up suitcase. I dragged it out and popped open the lid.

My new dummy lay inside the suitcase with his arms at his sides. He looked very dressy. He wore a black suit and a white shirt. He even had black suspenders and a red bow tie.

Big, black leather shoes were attached to the ends of his thin, dangling legs.

He had wavy red hair painted on top of his wooden head. His eyes were bright green, with big bushy eyebrows. His red painted lips curved up into an eerie smile.

7

He has a strange face, I thought. It was kind of intense. His eyes looked almost real. And he seemed to be grinning right at me!

His name — "Slappy" — had been painted in big letters inside the lid of the suitcase.

"Slappy! Oh wow, he's great!" I cried. "Daddy, thank you!" I kissed Dad on his forehead. Then I reached into the suitcase and carefully picked Slappy up. As I did, a small white card fell from his hand.

I picked up the card. "'Karru Marri odonna loma molonu karrano'?" I read. Then I shrugged. "Sounds like a foreign language or something."

"I know what it means," Jed piped up. "'It takes a dummy to want a dummy'!"

Big joke. I ignored Jed and hugged Slappy. "You and I are going to make a great team," I whispered into his ear. "I just know it!"

I hugged him even closer.

And as Slappy's head dropped over my shoulder, I got the weirdest feeling.

My new dummy felt almost alive!

2

Later that night, I took Slappy and Dennis to my bedroom. I propped up the old dummy on the bench by my window and stuck his head back on.

Then I changed into my PJs, picked up Slappy, and sat on my bed. With Slappy on my lap, I took hold of the string that worked his mouth. Then I stuck my finger inside his head and found the little lever to make his eyes move back and forth.

I was ready to practice!

"It's nice to meet you," I said to Slappy.

"It's nice to meet you, too, Amy," I answered for Slappy.

I gave Slappy a voice that was different from Dennis's. Lower and deeper. It sounded great. And it felt as if I didn't have to move my lips as much as I did with Dennis.

"It must be great to have a new home," I told Slappy.

His head turned. His green eyes snapped up and stared into my face.

Whoa! I thought. I guess it doesn't take much to turn his head. I barely touched him.

"You got that right, kiddo!" Slappy said.

"Amy?"

I glanced toward the door. Sara stood there, scowling at me. "Amy, about my sweater, if you come into my room again and I catch you, you're toast. Got it?" she snapped.

"I didn't hurt your dumb sweater!" I told her. "I was just trying it on."

"Well, just stay out," Sara ordered. "Now go to bed."

"Don't have to," I replied.

"Yeah, we don't have to," Slappy repeated.

Wow! I thought. I didn't move my lips at

all that time. I'm getting so good at this it's almost scary.

Sara frowned at both of us. "Come on, Mom says so," she told me. Then she left.

It was getting late. I placed Slappy on the bench across from Dennis.

"Look, Dennis. Here's your new friend, Slappy." After they looked at each other, I turned their heads so they both faced me. "Good night, Slappy. Good night, Dennis."

I turned off the light and crawled into bed. As I pulled up the cover, I heard a thud. I jumped out of bed and flipped the light back on.

And gasped.

Dennis lay sprawled on the floor in front of the window bench.

"Oh, Dennis!" I said with a groan. I crossed the room and tossed him back on the bench.

As I did, I noticed something. Dennis's head had been twisted around. It was on totally backward.

A little shiver ran down my spine.

How could that have happened?

"Nooo! Oh, nooo!"

A piercing scream echoed through the house.

I sat up and blinked. Bright morning light streamed through the curtains. I shoved back the covers and leaped out of bed.

"Mom! Dad!" a voice shrieked.

Sara's voice.

I raced down the hall. As I got close to Sara's room, I stepped on something. It felt like a pencil. I picked it up without even looking at it and ran into her room. Jed arrived right behind me. Mom and Dad were already there, in their bathrobes.

"Sara, what is it?" Mom wrapped her arm around my sister and tried to calm her down.

Sara wasn't scared. Her face was red with rage. "It's ruined!" she cried. "Just look. It's totally destroyed!"

Sara raised her arm and pointed to the easel in her room.

We all gasped.

On the easel sat Sara's "Home Sweet Home" painting.

On top of her painting somebody had drawn big, ugly stick figures — in bright red paint!

Jed rubbed his eyes and stared at my hand. "Amy, what did you do that for?" he asked me.

Everybody followed his gaze.

I glanced down at my hand.

"Oh, wow," I whispered. I couldn't believe what I saw.

In my hand was a paintbrush.

A paintbrush dripping with bright red paint!

3

We all stared at the paintbrush.

Then everyone looked at me.

"I didn't do it," I stammered. "I found the brush in the hall."

"How could you?" Sara asked angrily. "You're always jealous of my art."

"I didn't mess up your painting," I insisted. "Why would I?"

"So who did?" Sara demanded. "The tooth fairy?"

"Pretty dumb, Amy," Jed chimed in. "Even I wouldn't try and get away with something like that."

"Jed, stay out of this," Mom ordered.

Dad gave me one of his I'm-disappointed-in-you looks. "We'll talk about this later, Amy," he said. "Now go get dressed for school."

"I'm always blamed for *everything* around here!" I shouted. Then I turned and ran back to my room.

It took me forever to get dressed. As I gathered my books for school, Mom called from downstairs. "Amy, you'll miss your bus!"

"Coming!" I yelled back.

Mom had used her stern voice. I could tell she thought I had ruined Sara's painting.

But I hadn't! I had no idea how that paint-brush ended up in the hall. All I knew was that I hadn't done anything wrong. How come nobody believed me?

Before I left, I glanced at the bench by the window. Dennis sat where I had left him, his head sagging forward. He looked sort of sad.

Slappy sat in his corner, staring straight ahead.

15

I walked over to him. "Sorry you had to end up with such a bizarre family, Slappy."

I folded his hands on his lap and picked up my schoolbooks. That's when I noticed the paint. Red paint on my fingers.

"Oooh . . . red paint?" I wondered out loud. "What's going on?"

I looked back at Slappy. I looked at his hand.

There was red paint all over Slappy's right hand!

"How did you get paint on you?" I asked.

Slappy didn't answer, of course.

But for just a second, the grin on his red lips seemed wider.

And the sparkle in his green eyes looked even brighter.

Dad strummed a chord on his guitar. "If you're happy and you know it, clap your hands!" he sang.

The rest of the family clapped on cue.

It was Thursday night again. Family Night.

It was Dad's turn. He had almost finished. It would be my turn after that. I had practiced with Slappy all week, and I couldn't wait to show everyone how good I was.

"If you're happy and you know it and you really want to show it..." Dad sang on, strumming along on his guitar. He loved to play the guitar. He wasn't very good, but we'd never tell him that.

"If you're happy and you know it, clap your hands!" we all sang together.

Everyone clapped. I moved Slappy's hands back and forth as if he were clapping, too.

Dad took a bow. "Thank you. Thank you, ladies and germs," he said. "And now I'd like to turn the Family Night stage over to Amy Kramer and her little pal, Slappy! Take it away, Amy."

Everyone applauded. Jed whistled.

I adjusted Slappy on my knee and turned his head to look at the family.

"Hey there, family! Nice to see you," I said in my Slappy voice.

Then I turned Slappy's head to face me.

"So, Slappy, how do you like being part of the Kramer family so far?" I asked the dummy.

"It's fantastic!" Slappy declared. "But then, my last family was only a pine tree. Hah! Hah!"

Huh? I thought. Everyone groaned and chuckled at the joke, but the joke wasn't what I planned to make Slappy say! What was going on?

I cleared my throat. "So what did you think of Dad's song?" I asked the dummy.

Slappy's head swiveled quickly toward Dad.

"That was your dad?" he asked. "Well, what a relief. I thought the cat got stuck in the dishwasher! Heh-heh-heh-hah."

Jed burst out laughing. Sara giggled. Mom and Dad looked shocked by Slappy's nasty joke.

But they weren't as shocked as I was!

Because *I* hadn't made Slappy say the joke!

"Amy!" Mom scolded. "This isn't like you!"

"But it's not me! It's him!" I cried out.

It *was* Slappy. Talking on his own!

I tried to pull my hand out of the dummy's head, but I couldn't. My hand was stuck. "It's him!" I repeated.

"Oh, right! The dummy made me do it!" Jed rolled his eyes and laughed.

Slappy turned to Jed. "I wouldn't laugh," he told my brother. "You're such a booger-brain, you would try to grow an eggplant by burying a chicken!"

"Hey! Cut it out!" Jed shouted at me.

"Yeah! Cut it out!" I yelled at Slappy.

I stood up and pulled. I still couldn't get my hand free.

Then Slappy turned his head to Sara. "You call yourself an artist?" he asked with a sneer in his voice. "Why don't you give up brushes and try using a roller?"

My sister gave me a dirty look. "Is this supposed to be funny?"

"No! I can't stop him!" I tugged on Slappy's sleeve, still trying to get loose.

"Hey, easy on the threads!" Slappy yelled at me.

"Help me!" I pleaded. "I can't get him off!"

"Well, I can!" Sara declared angrily. She grabbed Slappy by the arm and yanked hard. She pulled and pulled. Finally Slappy came loose. My hand was free.

Sara threw the dummy on a chair.

"Amy, what has gotten into you?" Mom demanded.

"Hey kids, come on," Slappy interrupted. "Get a grip! Come on."

Slappy was jabbering!

Slappy was.

Not *me*!

"Mom, I'm not saying those things," I shouted. "Slappy is!"

Dad stood up, frowning. I could tell that he didn't believe me. "Okay, young lady, that's enough," he told me. "Up to bed."

Dad scooped Slappy off the chair and handed him to me. "And take the dummy with you," he ordered.

I turned and ran out of the living room. Blamed again for something I didn't do.

"I'm in big trouble because of you!" I yelled at the dummy as I went upstairs.

Slappy turned his head.

His green eyes stared straight into mine.

Then he laughed. A deep, hideous laugh that made me shiver.

"Heh-heh-heh-heh-hah-hah-hah!"

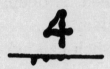

I didn't know *what* was going on!

All I knew was, I didn't want anything more to do with Slappy. He really creeped me out!

I stuck him in his suitcase and buried it deep in my closet, behind my Barbie dolls and stuffed animals.

I never wanted to see that weird dummy again.

A week after I threw Slappy in the closet, my best friend, Margo, came over. We were going to make a poster for the "Save the Rain Forest" dance on Friday night.

I had borrowed a bunch of my sister's colored markers.

Margo brought the poster board — and her six-year-old sister, Alicia.

While Margo and I worked on the poster, Alicia wandered around my bedroom, checking everything out.

"Wow, this poster's turning out great!" Margo said after a while. She added some more green to one of the trees.

"Yeah, you're right," I agreed. "So, do you think Shane's going to ask you to the dance?"

"I wish!" Margo answered, sighing. She has a major crush on Shane. "But I can always go with Tyler."

Margo sighed again. Then she glanced over her shoulder to check on her sister. "Alicia, what have you got there?" she asked.

"Dolls." Alicia sat just inside my closet. She held up one of the dolls. "I found them."

Margo rolled her eyes at me. "Sorry. She's such a snoop."

"That's okay," I told her. "It's not like I play with dolls anymore."

"How come I always get stuck baby-sitting?" Margo complained.

"It's because you're the one in the middle, like me," I explained. "The oldest kids get to do whatever they want. The youngest ones get away with everything. Being in the middle, you get stuck with everything. Sometimes I wish I didn't have any brothers or sisters."

"Yeah, tell me about it," Margo agreed.

"Amy!" an angry voice suddenly boomed out.

Margo and I jumped and turned to the door.

Sara stood there, her face the color of a tomato. She was furious.

Now what? I wondered.

"Who said you could go into my room and steal my markers?" Sara demanded.

"I didn't steal them," I told her. "We're just borrowing them."

"You never even asked!" Sara came in and grabbed the green marker right out of Margo's hand. Then she yanked the blue one from mine. "I told you to stay out of my room!"

Sara gathered the rest of her markers off the floor. Then she stormed out of the room.

"You stay out of my *life*!" I yelled at her.

When I turned back, I looked at Margo's little sister, and my heart almost stopped beating.

Alicia still sat in the closet doorway. An open suitcase lay on the floor next to her. And it wasn't a doll on her lap.

It was Slappy!

"Hi, Slappy," she said to the dummy. "My name is Alicia."

"Alicia! Don't touch that!" I called out.

"She won't hurt it, Amy," Margo said, standing up for her sister.

Alicia patted Slappy's wooden head. "He said he couldn't breathe in the suitcase," she explained.

I jumped up and hurried over to Alicia. I had to get Slappy away from her — back into his suitcase where he belonged!

The moment I grabbed hold of Slappy's skinny wooden body, his head whipped around toward Margo.

"Hey, Margo, you can forget about Shane!" Slappy told her. "He thinks you've got a face like a can of worms!"

"Amy!" Margo cried.

Alicia laughed.

"Stop it!" I yelled at Slappy.

"I didn't say that stuff about Shane," I told Margo, trying to explain. "*He* did!"

"Slappy's funny," Alicia said. She laughed again and took hold of Slappy's hand.

In a flash, Slappy's wooden fingers grabbed Alicia's hand.

"Ow!" Alicia cried out. She tried to yank her hand away. "Hey! He won't let me go!"

Slappy gave a frightening laugh. "Heh-heh-heh-hah-hah-hah!"

"Amy, cut it out. Stop it!" Margo shouted at me. "Let her go!"

"Let me go!" Alicia whimpered.

"Heh-heh-heh-hah-hah-hah-hah!" Slappy laughed.

Margo grabbed Slappy's hand and tried to pull his fingers open. But she couldn't budge them.

Then I tugged on his arm — as hard as I could. I couldn't pull him loose, either.

"Let me go!" Alicia cried hysterically. "Help!"

5

Alicia wailed.

Margo tugged.

I pulled.

But Slappy had Alicia's hand in an iron grip. And he wouldn't let go!

"Make him stop!" Alicia cried. "Make him stop!"

Margo grabbed my arm. "Amy, what are you doing?" she shouted at me.

"I'm not doing anything!" I yelled back.

"Slappy, stop it! Let her go!" I screamed at the dummy.

Mom burst into the room as I was screaming at Slappy.

"What in the world?" she gasped.

My name is Amy Kramer. I'm a ventriloquist. But it's hard to be a good ventriloquist when your dummy's head keeps falling off.

One day, my dad brought home Slappy—a new dummy. I thought Slappy was the coolest.

"You and I are going to make a great team," I whispered in his ear. Boy, was I wrong.

I sat Slappy next to my old dummy, Dennis. In the morning I found Dennis on the floor!

I discovered that Slappy was different. He was *alive*! And he was *evil*! And he wanted to get me into trouble—big trouble!

First, he destroyed my sister's favorite painting—and I got blamed for that.

He made my friend's little sister cry. He grabbed her hand tightly, and wouldn't let her go! I got blamed for that, too!

Then I caught Slappy with Dad's guitar. He was about to smash it over Dad's head! There was no way I was going to take the blame again, so...

...I tackled Slappy to the floor. But I landed on Dad's guitar. Dad woke up and saw me on the floor with his guitar—his totally smashed guitar—and blamed me.

That's it! I said to myself. *Slappy has to go.* My sister and I searched for him in the dark. We planned a surprise attack. But we were the ones in for a surprise.

Suddenly Slappy let go of Alicia's hand. His arm dropped limply by his side.

I grabbed Slappy and threw him on my bed. Then I ran back to Alicia.

"Are you all right?" I asked.

"Stay away from her, Amy!" Margo yelled.

"What is going on up here?" Mom asked.

"Slappy grabbed Alicia and he wouldn't let go!" I told her.

"What?" Mom looked annoyed with me.

"Amy, you are such a liar!" Margo fumed. "A big, fat liar."

Margo grabbed her sister's hand and pulled her toward the door. "I don't ever want to see you again!" she shouted at me over her shoulder. "Not ever!"

"Margo, it wasn't me!" I cried.

Margo ignored me and rushed out the door. I ran after her. "Margo, it wasn't me!" I shouted as she and Alicia hurried down the stairs.

I started to run down the stairs, but Mom grabbed my shoulder. "Amy! This has gone far enough!" she told me.

"But . . ." I started to argue.

Mom held up her hand to stop me. "You are staying in your room until your father gets home!" she ordered. "I don't want to hear another word about that dummy!"

She left my room and pulled the door shut.

"Hah, hah, hah!" a sneering laugh came from the bed.

I spun around.

"Hah, hah, hah . . . ahah, hah, hah!" Slappy laughed more and more wildly.

I stared at him in horror.

This couldn't be happening!

"Amy, this isn't funny," Dad said in a serious voice.

He had asked everybody in the family to come into the living room that night to talk. I sat alone on one couch, while Mom, Dad, Sara, and Jed sat around and stared at me.

Sara looked sort of annoyed. Jed looked as if he were trying to keep from laughing.

Mom wasn't angry anymore. But she and Dad both had worried looks on their faces.

I felt like some kind of alien from another planet.

"It has to stop," Dad went on. "You can't keep blaming a doll for things you don't want to take responsibility for."

"Slappy's not a doll. He's a dummy," I replied. "And I can't help it if he's haunted or something. Why won't anybody believe me?"

Dad stood up and began to pace up and down. Obviously he didn't know what to say.

Sara frowned at me. "Amy, this is getting too weird."

"Weird with a capital *W*," Jed added.

"Come on now, you two," Mom told them. "We're here as a family to help Amy — not to criticize."

Sara rolled her eyes. "Yeah, right."

I sat up straight on the couch. "I know it's hard to believe," I said, "but something's going on that I can't stop. Something I can't explain."

Dad shook his head. "Pumpkin, when I was your age, I had two older brothers plus a baby sister to deal with," he told me. He rubbed his bald spot and smiled at me. "I know what it feels like to be caught in the middle."

I jumped to my feet. "Nobody's listening to me!" I cried. "It's all Slappy's fault!"

Mom sighed. "Amy, if you really and truly believe that Slappy's responsible for all this, then maybe we need to get you some help."

"You mean . . . like a doctor or something?" I asked.

"Like a total headshrinker!" Sara declared.

"Sara!" Dad gave my sister a warning look.

"I'm not making this up!" I shouted.

But I was wasting my breath. I could tell nobody believed me.

I bolted from the living room and ran up the stairs.

Nobody came after me.

They all think I'm lying, I thought as I closed myself in my room.

But I'm not lying.

I'm not!

*   *   *

I shut Slappy away in the closet again. Then I climbed into bed. The wind outside blew tree branches against the side of the house and made creepy shadows on the walls.

I pulled the covers over my head.

I tried not to think about Slappy. Or my family. Or how they thought I made everything up.

I tossed and turned for a long time, but finally I fell asleep.

A blast of cold air woke me up. It was still dark.

I bolted up in bed, groggy with sleep.

The cool wind blew across my face. I shivered and glanced around. I'd forgotten to close the window.

I rubbed my eyes and swung my legs to the floor. As I did, I noticed something.

The closet door was open. I knew I had shut it when I threw Slappy in the closet, but now the door was open.

Slappy's suitcase stood on the floor by the door. It was open, too!

And Slappy wasn't in it!

My eyes darted around the room.

No Slappy.

He escaped! I thought.

I jumped out of bed and ran into the hall-way. I didn't see anything. But I could hear the TV on downstairs in the living room.

I raced downstairs to the living room and skidded to a stop.

Mom and Dad were on the couch. They'd both fallen asleep in front of the television.

Slappy stood right in front of my father. In his little hands, he held Dad's wooden guitar.

Slowly Slappy raised the guitar into the air.

I gasped in horror.

Slappy was going to bash Dad in the head with his own guitar!

6

Slappy turned toward me.

The painted eyes glared.

His face wore a horrible grin of pure evil.

Slappy grunted. He turned back to Dad and raised the guitar even higher.

There was only one thing to do — grab the guitar!

I charged into the room and tackled the dummy. His head hit the floor with a *thunk*.

Next I heard the crunch of wood. And a twanging sound.

All the noise woke Mom and Dad. They opened their eyes and blinked.

"What in the . . . ?" Dad mumbled sleepily. Then his eyes widened. So did Mom's.

Both of them sat up and stared.

What were they looking at?

Me. Holding Dad's crushed guitar!

"Oh, Amy, how could you?" Mom gasped.

"He was going to hit Dad," I blurted out. "I had to stop him!"

Dad looked confused. "Stop who?" he asked. "What are you talking about?"

I looked at Slappy. He was lying on the floor, playing dead. The smile on his wooden face made him look sweet and innocent.

I glanced back at my parents. Their expressions were a mixture of anger and sadness.

They still don't believe me, I thought.

"Amy —" Mom started to say.

"I didn't do it!" I interrupted. My eyes filled with tears. "Slappy did!"

Dad stood up. "Okay, this stops here and now!" he told me. He tried to keep his voice calm, but I could tell he was really angry.

"But . . . but . . ." I tried to say something, but Dad wouldn't let me.

"No buts, young lady." He pointed to the door. "I want you back upstairs and in bed — now! We'll discuss this in the morning."

As I left, I glanced back and saw Mom pick Slappy up off the floor.

The dummy stayed totally limp.

And he still had that innocent smile on his face. The smile that said "I didn't do anything."

Yeah, right! I thought.

Let's just say that I wasn't looking forward to breakfast the next morning.

The second I walked into the kitchen, Jed stopped inhaling his pancakes and gave a nervous laugh.

Sara glanced up from the table and scowled at me.

Mom was getting ready for work. She's a real estate agent. She put on her company jacket and tossed her cell phone into her briefcase. Mom gave me a worried look, but didn't say anything.

Jed went back to eating. "Way to go, Amy!" he cracked with his mouth full.

"Oh, be quiet!" I yelled at him as I sat down. "I never did anything!"

Then Dad came into the kitchen. He didn't look happy.

He's definitely still angry about last night, I thought. Suddenly I didn't feel hungry anymore.

"Jed, Sara, get ready for school," Dad ordered.

"I *am* ready," Jed protested.

"They want to talk to Amy alone," Sara told him. She grabbed Jed's arm and dragged him out of the kitchen.

"Amy, your mother and I have talked about this situation," Dad began.

I stared at my plate and kept quiet.

"And we want you to tell us what you think we should do," Dad continued.

"You mean like punishment?" I asked, still looking down at my breakfast.

Mom zipped up her briefcase. "I think we all know that's not the answer," she said.

"This is about a lot more than wrecking your father's guitar."

I tried to think of something to say. But I couldn't come up with anything except the truth.

And they didn't believe that!

"Amy, we want to help." Dad's voice was soft. He sounded concerned. "But we can't begin to understand what's happening here if you keep blaming Slappy for everything."

"I'm telling the truth," I whispered.

I raised my head and looked them in the eyes.

Mom and Dad stared back at me. Then they exchanged disappointed glances.

Mom sighed. "I'm late for an open house." She tucked her briefcase under her arm and left the kitchen.

Dad turned to me. "When you're ready to tell us what's really bothering you, then we'll talk," he told me. "Is that clear?"

I nodded.

But I knew it would be a long time before we talked.

Maybe even forever.

Because I already told them what was really bothering me.

And they didn't believe me.

After I left the kitchen, I came up with a plan. It was up to me to figure out an answer fast, or Mom and Dad would do something really crazy.

What was the answer?

I had to get rid of Slappy.

I went up to my room and tossed the dummy into a laundry bag. Then I grabbed my schoolbooks and headed for the bus stop.

On the way, I saw Margo with two other girls, Cindy Ryan and Jill Carlson. They were tacking a "Save the Rain Forest" dance poster to a telephone pole.

"This is going to be a really cool dance," Cindy said as I got closer.

"Yeah," Jill answered. "Let's put up one more sign here. Then we'll go to the next block."

"Hi, Margo!" I called out as I walked by.

Margo didn't say a word! She didn't even look at me. She just walked away with Cindy and Jill. I felt totally invisible.

I watched as they began tacking up another dance poster. I wanted to cry. Slappy was ruining my life!

I blinked back the tears and kept walking. Everything will be all right, I told myself. Just as soon as I get rid of Slappy, things will be normal again.

When the three girls were out of sight, I stopped and glanced around.

The coast was clear.

I put the laundry bag on the ground and opened it.

Slappy stared up at me with his evil grin.

"You're never going to hurt me again," I told him. "Not ever!"

I pulled the dummy from the bag.

Then I stuffed him headfirst through a sewer grate!

That night I washed the dishes after dinner. I felt fantastic.

Slappy's gone for good! I thought.

The evil dummy is out of our lives!

"Amy, I have to ask you something," Sara said. She was on the kitchen floor wiping up muddy little footprints. "Why did you do it, really?"

"Do what?" I asked, as if I didn't know what she was talking about.

"Wreck Dad's guitar," Sara told me. She went back to wiping the floor. "You knew you couldn't get away with it."

I dried off a couple of forks. "There's no point in my telling you the truth because you won't believe me," I told her. "You think I'm crazy."

Sara didn't say anything.

I'm right, I thought. She does think I'm crazy!

That made me mad. I tossed the dishcloth on the counter and headed for the door.

"When you get upstairs, tell Jed to wipe his stupid feet!" Sara called after me.

I didn't bother to answer. I just grabbed my books off the counter and ran upstairs.

When I got to my room, I tossed my books on the bed and started to pull off my sneakers. As I did, I noticed something strange.

More muddy footprints on the floor.

Footprints leading under my bed!

A chill ran down my spine as I stared at the trail of shoe prints.

It's just Jed, I told myself. He's fooling around. Playing some kind of joke on me.

But I had to make sure.

Slowly, I got down on my hands and knees and lifted the bedspread.

I took a deep breath and peered under the bed.

Nothing but darkness.

Thank goodness! I thought. With a sigh of relief, I dropped the bedspread and turned around.

"Oh, no!" I gasped.

7

Slappy sat on the floor behind me, grinning his hideous grin.

"Hey, Amy. Guess who?" he said. Then the dummy's mouth dropped open as he began to cackle. "Heh-heh-heh-heh . . ."

My heart pounded. I scooted back against the bed.

"Keep away from me!" I warned.

"But we're partners, Amy, remember?" Slappy teased in his deep voice. "It wasn't very nice of you to dump me in the sewer like that."

"Wha-what do you want?" I stammered.

Slappy's big eyes glared at me. "Don't you

get it yet?" he teased. "You can't get rid of me."

"What are you talking about?" I cried.

"Don't you remember, Amy?" the dummy went on. "You spoke the words: Karru Marri odonna loma . . ."

". . . molonu karrano," I whispered, finishing the strange saying.

Slappy's evil grin widened. "The words mean you and I are one now. Inseparable. And you are my slave."

"No, I'm not going to be your slave!" I insisted. "You can't make me."

Slappy shook his head. "I can make you do anything I want! You have no choice. Your family already thinks you're crazy. I've seen to that."

I was afraid of the insane dummy, but I was also angry. I scooted up onto the bed and grabbed a pillow. Then I threw it across the room at Slappy as hard as I could.

Slappy leaned to one side. The pillow whizzed by him and hit the wall.

"Hah-hah-hah-hah!" he cackled. "They'll lock you up, Amy! Maybe your family will come see you on visiting days."

"No!" I shouted. Furious, I lunged at the dummy and knocked him to the floor.

"Whoa! Amy!" Slappy cried, sitting up again. "I can hurt you and your family in a hundred ways."

"No!" I screamed. "I won't let you!"

Slappy leaped to his feet and charged at me.

I screamed and jumped aside.

As I did, the door flew open. Sara burst into the room. "Amy?" she cried out.

"Sara!" I ran to my sister, shaking with fright.

"Amy, what are you —" Sara started to say.

"Sara, look!" I interrupted, pointing to Slappy. "He's . . . he's . . . he's . . ."

I couldn't find the words. But I didn't need to.

Sara's eyes widened. Her jaw dropped. She saw Slappy move.

Slappy, the wooden dummy, was moving around my bedroom on his own!

He turned his hideous smile on her.

"Hey, Sara!" he cried. "Wanna play?"

Sara screamed.

I screamed.

Then the lights went out.

Sara and I stood together, clutching each other in the darkness.

"Hey!" Jed called from downstairs. "What's going on?"

I started to answer him, but I clamped my lips together. If Slappy heard me, he'd know where we were.

Sara and I couldn't see the dummy. It was too dark. But we could hear him, muttering to himself. And moving around.

Then he started coming closer and closer to us.

"Run!" I cried.

Sara and I dashed out the door together.

Behind us I heard Slappy's terrible laugh. "Hah! Hah! Hah! You can run, but you can't hide. Hah! Hah! Hah!"

I screamed again.

Sara and I raced down the hallway and locked ourselves in the bathroom.

We put our ears to the door.

Silence.

We kept listening. And waiting.

"What are we going to do?" I finally whispered to Sara.

Sara shook her head. "I can't believe it," she muttered. "I just can't believe it!"

Suddenly we heard little footsteps. It was Slappy. He was pacing back and forth in the hallway.

He was right outside the bathroom door!

We pulled back and screamed again.

"Ready or not? Heh-heh-heh . . ." Slappy cackled.

The doorknob rattled.

Slappy was trying to get in.

Trying to get us!

I knew Sara finally realized I'd been telling the truth. "See?" I said to her, trying not to cry. "I told you. No one would believe me!"

Sara put her arms around me and gave me a hug. "I'm sorry! I believe you now," she whispered.

Slappy kept pacing outside the door. Pacing and laughing his crazed laugh.

Finally the sound of Slappy's feet disappeared. We heard no sounds from the other side of the door.

"I think he's gone," I whispered to Sara.

But where did he go? I wondered. Sara and I were quiet together in the dark. Then it hit us both at the same time.

Jed.

"Jed!" Sara yelled.

We opened the bathroom door and tried to see into the dark hallway.

No Slappy.

We tiptoed slowly down the hallway and toward the stairs.

I held onto Sara as she gripped the banister to guide her down the steps.

We made it safely to the bottom of the stairs.

It was pitch-black.

Clutching each other, Sara and I groped our way to the kitchen.

"Jed! Jed, where are you?" I called out.

No answer.

Sara let go of my hand. I could hear her banging into things in the dark. I heard a kitchen drawer slide open. Then a beam of light shot across the room.

Sara had found a flashlight. The light was dim. She shone it around the kitchen.

No Jed.

But I spotted the kitchen mop and grabbed it. A weapon! Now I was ready for Slappy.

Sara's dull flashlight helped a little as we slowly walked down the hallway to the dark living room.

"Jed?" Sara whispered in a shaky voice.

Silence.

Then came a loud crash.

We screamed.

Sara flashed the light. A lamp had fallen.

Then we heard that familiar laugh in the darkness.

"Heh-heh-heh."

I spun around.

"Yoo-hoo! Looking for somebody?" Slappy's voice taunted me.

I gazed around the living room. Finally, I spotted the dummy's shadowy figure up above us.

Slappy sat on top of the chandelier, staring down at me with an evil gleam in his eyes.

I took a step toward him, raised the mop above my head, and swung!

The mop swooshed through the air, missing the dummy.

Slappy cackled. "I've seen better swings on the playground!" he joked. Still laughing, he jumped down from the chandelier.

I heard him land. But I couldn't see him anymore.

"Where is he?" Sara shouted.

"I don't know!" I yelled.

Sara walked around the room slowly, flashing the light everywhere. I followed close behind. I kept the mop cocked above my head, ready to swing.

Suddenly a hand shot out of the darkness and grabbed my ankle.

I pulled away, then stumbled. As I fell, the mop flew out of my hands. It skidded across the floor to the other side of the room.

"Gotcha!" Slappy crowed.

"Amy?" Sara yelled out in terror.

Slappy leaped onto the coffee table. Then he began to move closer and closer to me. I couldn't get up off the floor. I was too scared.

"From now on this family belongs to me!" Slappy cackled.

I tried to scream, but nothing came out.

Slappy kept coming. His evil grin gleamed through the darkness.

"You're mine, Amy. You're mine!" Slappy laughed as he came closer.

It's all over, I thought. It's all over!

Suddenly someone burst out of nowhere and tackled Slappy from behind.

The dummy went flying into the fireplace.

His wooden head smashed into the bricks and split open.

I gasped.

A bright cloud of green light seeped from the dummy's cracked head. It lit up the room for a moment. Then, with a loud whoosh, the green light was sucked up the chimney.

"What was that?" Sara cried.

I didn't know. But I couldn't have answered anyway. I was shaking too hard.

"What's going on here?" It was Dad's voice calling out from the doorway. "Why are the lights out?"

I could see Mom and Dad standing together, peering into the darkness.

Sara and I rushed over to them. "Boy, are we glad to see you!" I cried.

"Amy was telling the truth!" Sara burst out excitedly. "Slappy came after us. He turned out the lights."

"But Jed saved us!" I said.

"What?" Mom interrupted. "Could you please slow down?"

"Yeah, slow down," a groggy voice said from behind me.

I spun around to see Jed standing at the bottom of the staircase.

"Jed!" I cried. Sara gasped.

"What's going on?" Jed asked, yawning. "What did I do?"

I stared at him. I thought Jed had tackled Slappy. But obviously he had just woken up. That meant Jed must have gone upstairs and fallen asleep after the lights went out.

I kept staring at my brother. "If you didn't stop Slappy, then who did?" I asked.

No one spoke. Sara shined the flashlight all around the room.

She stopped when she came to the coffee table.

A small figure stood on top of it.

The figure wore an old red turtleneck sweater.

The paint on its wooden face was faded, and its shaggy brown hair was a mess.

My old ventriloquist's dummy gazed at us for a second.

Then it grinned.

"Huh-huh," Dennis laughed. "It's good to be back in the family again. Ah-huh-huh-huh!"

GET
Goosebumps®
by R.L. Stine

❑ BAB45365-3	#1	Welcome to Dead House	$3.99
❑ BAB45366-1	#2	Stay Out of the Basement	$3.99
❑ BAB45367-X	#3	Monster Blood	$3.99
❑ BAB45368-8	#4	Say Cheese and Die!	$3.99
❑ BAB45369-6	#5	The Curse of the Mummy's Tomb	$3.99
❑ BAB49445-7	#10	The Ghost Next Door	$3.99
❑ BAB49450-3	#15	You Can't Scare Me!	$3.99
❑ BAB47742-0	#20	The Scarecrow Walks at Midnight	$3.99
❑ BAB47743-9	#21	Go Eat Worms!	$3.99
❑ BAB47744-7	#22	Ghost Beach	$3.99
❑ BAB47745-5	#23	Return of the Mummy	$3.99
❑ BAB48354-4	#24	Phantom of the Auditorium	$3.99
❑ BAB48355-2	#25	Attack of the Mutant	$3.99
❑ BAB48350-1	#26	My Hairiest Adventure	$3.99
❑ BAB48351-X	#27	A Night in Terror Tower	$3.99
❑ BAB48352-8	#28	The Cuckoo Clock of Doom	$3.99
❑ BAB48347-1	#29	Monster Blood III	$3.99
❑ BAB48348-X	#30	It Came from Beneath the Sink	$3.99
❑ BAB48349-8	#31	The Night of the Living Dummy II	$3.99
❑ BAB48344-7	#32	The Barking Ghost	$3.99
❑ BAB48345-5	#33	The Horror at Camp Jellyjam	$3.99
❑ BAB48346-3	#34	Revenge of the Lawn Gnomes	$3.99
❑ BAB48340-4	#35	A Shocker on Shock Street	$3.99
❑ BAB56873-6	#36	The Haunted Mask II	$3.99
❑ BAB56874-4	#37	The Headless Ghost	$3.99
❑ BAB56875-2	#38	The Abominable Snowman of Pasadena	$3.99
❑ BAB56876-0	#39	How I Got My Shrunken Head	$3.99
❑ BAB56877-9	#40	Night of the Living Dummy III	$3.99
❑ BAB56878-7	#41	Bad Hare Day	$3.99
❑ BAB56879-5	#42	Egg Monsters from Mars	$3.99
❑ BAB56880-9	#43	The Beast from the East	$3.99
❑ BAB56881-7	#44	Say Cheese and Die–Again!	$3.99
❑ BAB56882-5	#45	Ghost Camp	$3.99
❑ BAB56883-3	#46	How to Kill a Monster	$3.99
❑ BAB56884-1	#47	Legend of the Lost Legend	$3.99
❑ BAB56885-X	#48	Attack of the Jack-O'-Lanterns	$3.99

GOOSEBUMPS PRESENTS

❑ BAB74586-7	Goosebumps Presents TV Episode #1 The Girl Who Cried Monster	$3.99
❑ BAB74587-5	Goosebumps Presents TV Episode #2 The Cuckoo Clock of Doom	$3.99
❑ BAB74588-3	Goosebumps Presents TV Episode #3 Welcome to Camp Nightmare	$3.99
❑ BAB74589-1	Goosebumps Presents TV Episode #4 Return of the Mummy	$3.99

❑ BAB62836-4	Tales to Give You Goosebumps Book & Light Set Special Edition #1	$11.95
❑ BAB26603-9	More Tales to Give You Goosebumps Book & Light Set Special Edition #2	$11.95
❑ BAB74150-4	Even More Tales to Give You Goosebumps Book and Boxer Shorts Pack Special Edition #3	$14.99

GIVE YOURSELF GOOSEBUMPS

❑ BAB55323-2	Give Yourself Goosebumps #1: Escape from the Carnival of Horrors	$3.99
❑ BAB56645-8	Give Yourself Goosebumps #2: Tick Tock, You're Dead	$3.99
❑ BAB56646-6	Give Yourself Goosebumps #3: Trapped in Bat Wing Hall	$3.99
❑ BAB67318-1	Give Yourself Goosebumps #4: The Deadly Experiments of Dr. Eeek	$3.99
❑ BAB67319-X	Give Yourself Goosebumps #5: Night in Werewolf Woods	$3.99
❑ BAB67320-3	Give Yourself Goosebumps #6: Beware of the Purple Peanut Butter	$3.99
❑ BAB67321-1	Give Yourself Goosebumps #7: Under the Magician's Spell	$3.99
❑ BAB84765-1	Give Yourself Goosebumps #8: The Curse of the Creeping Coffin	$3.99
❑ BAB84766-X	Give Yourself Goosebumps #9: The Knight in Screaming Armor	$3.99
❑ BAB84767-8	Give Yourself Goosebumps #10: Diary of a Mad Mummy	$3.99

❑ BAB53770-9	The Goosebumps Monster Blood Pack	$11.95
❑ BAB50995-0	The Goosebumps Monster Edition #1	$12.95
❑ BAB93371-X	The Goosebumps Monster Edition #2	$12.95
❑ BAB60265-9	Goosebumps Official Collector's Caps Collecting Kit	$5.99
❑ BAB73906-9	Goosebumps Postcard Book	$7.95
❑ BAB73902-6	The 1997 Goosebumps 365 Scare-a-Day Calendar	$8.95
❑ BAB73907-7	The Goosebumps 1997 Wall Calendar	$10.99

Scare me, thrill me, mail me GOOSEBUMPS now!

Available wherever you buy books, or use this order form. Scholastic Inc., P.O. Box 7502,
2931 East McCarty Street, Jefferson City, MO 65102

Please send me the books I have checked above. I am enclosing $_____ (please add
$2.00 to cover shipping and handling). Send check or money order — no cash or C.O.D.s please.

Name _____Age _____

Address _____

City _____State/Zip _____

Please allow four to six weeks for delivery. Offer good in the U.S. only. Sorry, mail orders are not available to
residents of Canada. Prices subject to change.

GB496